A Spider's Web

Katie Smythe

Rosen REAL READERS

Rosen Classroom™
New York

A spider makes silk
to build a web.
It builds a web
to catch bugs.

A spider puts silk
onto a plant.
This is where
he will build his web.

A spider makes a
Y shape with silk.
This will hold the web in place.

A spider adds more lines
to the Y shape.
He moves in circles
to fill the web.

A spider works hard
to build a web.

He waits for bugs
to fly into the web.

A bee flies into the web.

The bee is stuck.

It cannot get out.

The spider wraps
the bee in silk.
He bites the bee.
The bee dies.

The spider is hungry.

He eats the bee.

Sometimes a web breaks.
The spider must leave the web.
He looks for a place
to build a new web.

Words to Know

bee

plant

silk

spider